C701682687

D1337070

For my family

~S C

For Jim and Raechele

~J T

LITTLE TIGER PRESS
1 The Coda Centre, 189 Munster Road,
London SW6 6AW
www.littletiger.co.uk
First published in Great Britain 2000
This edition published 2013
Text copyright © Sheridan Cain 2000
Illustrations copyright © Jack Tickle 2000
Visit Jack Tickle at www.ChapmanandWarnes.com
Sheridan Cain and Jack Tickle have asserted
their rights to be identified as the author
and illustrator of this work under the
Copyright, Designs and Patents Act, 1988
Printed in China • LTP/1800/0613/0513
All rights reserved
ISBN 978-1-84895-737-4
2 4 6 8 10 9 7 5 3 1

South Lanarkshire Library Service	
LN	
C701682687	
Askews & Holts	
JN	£4.99
4425571	

The Crunching Munching Caterpillar

Sheridan Cain

Jack Tickle

LITTLE TIGER PRESS
London

Caterpillar was always hungry.
For weeks he crunched and munched
his way through the fresh,
juicy leaves of a blackberry bush.

Bzzzzzzzz

One day, Caterpillar was about to crunch into another leaf when . . .

"Wow!" said Caterpillar,
"how did you get here?"
    "Simple," said Bumblebee,
"I have wings. Look!"
    "Oh, I'd like some of those,"
said Caterpillar.

Bumblebee flew up into the air and buzzed busily from flower to flower.

Bzzz_{zz}
Bzzz_{zz}

"I'd love to fly like that," said Caterpillar.
"Well, you can't," said Bumblebee. "I've got wings, and you've got legs. Your legs are for walking."
"I guess so," sighed Caterpillar.

Bzzzzzoommm

Bumblebee flew off to the next bush. Watching Bumblebee fly had made Caterpillar very hungry, so he crunched and he munched until it was time for bed.

crunch
Munch
yaw-w-n!

Caterpillar woke to
the sound of twittering.
Birds swooped and soared
in the early morning light.

Caterpillar was just about
to start his breakfast when . . .

. . . Sparrow landed
beside him.

"I'd love to fly high
in the air like that,"
said Caterpillar.
"Well, you can't," said Sparrow.
"You need to be as light as the
dandelion clock that floats on
the breeze."

"I guess so," said Caterpillar glumly.

Caterpillar carried on
crunch-munching all day,
until the light began to dim.

He wrapped a leaf around
himself to keep warm.
He was just about to
go to sleep when . . .

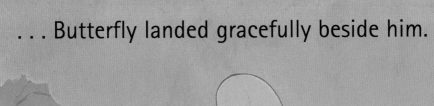

. . . Butterfly landed gracefully beside him.

"Oh, I wish I could fly like you," sighed
Caterpillar. "But I'm too fat and I have
legs instead of wings."

Butterfly smiled a secret, knowing smile.
"Who knows? Perhaps one day you will fly,
light as a feather, like me," she said. "But
now, little Caterpillar, you should go
to sleep. You look very tired."

Butterfly was right. Caterpillar
suddenly felt very sleepy.
As Butterfly flew off into
the night sky, he fell
into a deep, deep sleep.

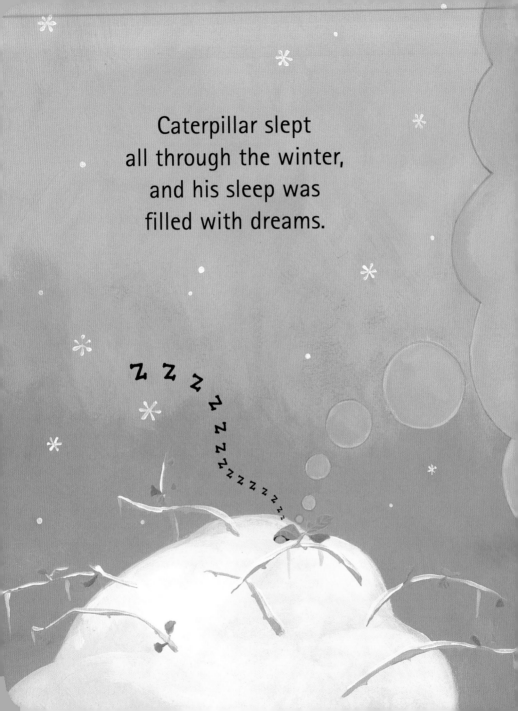

Caterpillar slept
all through the winter,
and his sleep was
filled with dreams.

Z Z Z Z Z Z Z Z Z Z Z Z Z Z Z Z Z Z Z

He dreamed he had wings and was soaring in the blue sky above the tall trees . . . .

He dreamed he was a dandelion clock, drifting towards the sun.

He dreamed he was as light as a feather, floating on the breeze.

When Caterpillar woke up he felt
the warmth of the spring sun.
He was stiff from his long sleep,
but he did not feel very hungry.

He **stretched** and **stretched** . . .

. . . and a breeze lifted
Caterpillar into the air.

He was no longer
short and plump.
He had WINGS!
Great, big, wonderful
BUTTERFLY WINGS!

"Wow!" said Young Butterfly.
"I'm flying! I'm really flying!"